To: Brittany

From: Aunt Joy & Uncle Joe

Christmas 1992

This book belongs to

_____

Mother Goose's Nursery Rhymes

ILLUSTRATED BY

Robyn Officer

ARIEL BOOKS

ANDREWS AND McMEEL

KANSAS CITY

Library of Congress Cataloging-in-Publication Data

Mother Goose.
      Mother Goose's nursery rhymes / illustrated by Robyn Officer.
          p.   cm.
      "Ariel Books."
      Summary: An illustrated collection of traditional rhymes.
      ISBN 0–8362–4907–0 : $6.95
      1. Nursery rhymes. 2. Children's poetry. [1. Nursery rhymes.]
  I. Officer, Robyn, ill. II. Title.
  PZ8.3.M85   1991c   91–2909
                                                                 CIP
                                                                  AC

Design: Susan Hood and Mike Hortens
Art Direction: Armand Eisen, Mike Hortens, and Julie Phillips
Art Production: Lynn Wine
Production: Julie Miller and Lisa Shadid

Mother Goose's
Nursery Rhymes

*H*ERE WE GO *round the mulberry bush,*
The mulberry bush, the mulberry bush.
Here we go round the mulberry bush,
On a cold and frosty morning.

*H*ICKORY, dickory, dock,
The mouse ran up the clock.
The clock struck one,
The mouse ran down,
And hickory, dickory, dock.

*L*ITTLE BO-PEEP has lost her sheep,
And doesn't know where to find them.
Leave them alone, and they'll come home,
Dragging their tails behind them.

*S*IMPLE SIMON *met a pieman*
Going to the fair;
Says Simple Simon to the pieman,
Let me taste your ware.

Says the pieman to Simple Simon,
Show me first your penny.
Says Simple Simon to the pieman,
Indeed I have not any.

*H*EY Diddle, Diddle,
The cat and the fiddle,
The cow jumped over the moon;
The little dog laughed
To see such sport
And the dish ran away with the spoon.

*J*ACK SPRAT could eat no fat,
  His wife could eat no lean;
And so, betwixt them both, you see,
They licked the platter clean.

THIS LITTLE PIGGY *went to market,*
This little piggy stayed home;
This little piggy had roast beef,
This little piggy had none,
And this little piggy cried wee-wee-wee all the
   way home.

$\mathcal{I}$TSY bitsy spider, climbed up the water spout,
Down came the rain and washed poor spider out.
Out came the sun and dried up all the rain;
And the itsy bitsy spider, climbed up the spout
  again.

$\mathcal{R}$ING around the roses,
A pocket full of posies;
Ashes, ashes!
We all fall down.

CHREE blind mice, see how they run!
They all ran after the farmer's wife,
Who cut off their tails with a carving knife.
Did you ever see such a sight in your life,
As three blind mice?

*H*UMPTY *D*UMPTY *sat on a wall,*
Humpty Dumpty had a great fall.
All the king's horses and all the king's men
Couldn't put Humpty Dumpty together again.

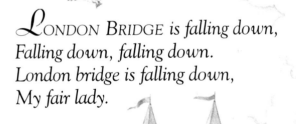

*L*ONDON *B*RIDGE *is falling down,*
Falling down, falling down.
London bridge is falling down,
My fair lady.

Little Boy Blue, come blow your horn,
The sheep's in the meadow, the cow's in the corn.
But where is the little boy who looks after the
*   sheep?*
He's under the haystack fast asleep.
Will you wake him? No, not I,
For if I do, he's sure to cry.

*S*TAR LIGHT, *star bright,*
First star I see tonight,
I wish I may, I wish I might,
Have the wish I wish tonight.

*J*ACK *be nimble,*
Jack be quick,
Jack jump over
The candlestick.

$\mathscr{P}$USSY CAT, *pussy cat, where have you been?*
I've been to London to look at the queen.
Pussy cat, pussy cat, what did you there?
I frightened a little mouse under her chair.

*P*AT-A-CAKE, pat-a-cake, baker's man,
Bake me a cake as fast as you can.
Pat it and prick it, and mark it with a T,
Put it in the oven for Tommy and me.

*O*LD Mother Hubbard
Went to the cupboard
To fetch her poor dog a bone,
But when she got there
The cupboard was bare
And so the poor dog had none.

21

*T*HERE WAS *an old woman who lived in a
shoe,
She had so many children she didn't know what
to do;
She gave them some broth without any bread;
She whipped them all soundly and put them to
bed.*

*J*ACK *and Jill went up the hill
To fetch a pail of water;
Jack fell down and broke his crown,
And Jill came tumbling after.*

$\mathcal{P}$ETER PIPER picked a peck of pickled pepper
A peck of pickled pepper Peter Piper picked.
If Peter Piper picked a peck of pickled pepper,
Where's the peck of pickled pepper Peter Piper
    picked?

$\mathcal{T}$OM, TOM, *the piper's son,*
Stole a pig and away did run;
The pig was eat, and Tom was beat,
And Tom ran crying down the street.

$\mathcal{R}$UB-a-dub-dub,
Three men in a tub,
And who do you think they be?
The butcher, the baker,
The candlestick-maker,
Turn 'em out, knaves all three!

*M*ARY had a little lamb,
Its fleece was white as snow;
And everywhere that Mary went
The lamb was sure to go.

It followed her to school one day,
That was against the rule;
It made the children laugh and play,
To see a lamb in school.

*P*ETER, PETER, *pumpkin eater,*
Had a wife and couldn't keep her;
He put her in a pumpkin shell,
And there he kept her very well.

Peter, Peter, pumpkin eater,
Had another, and didn't love her;
Peter learned to read and spell,
And then he loved her very well.

*T*WINKLE, *twinkle, little star*
How I wonder where you are!
Up above the world so high,
Like a diamond in the sky.

*S*LEEP, *baby, sleep,*
Thy father guards the sheep;
Thy mother shakes the dreamland tree,
And from it fall sweet dreams for thee.
Sleep, baby, sleep.

THERE WAS a crooked man,
And he walked a crooked mile,
He found a crooked sixpence
Against a crooked stile;
He bought a crooked cat,
Which caught a crooked mouse,
And they all lived together
In a little crooked house.

OLD King Cole
Was a merry old soul,
And a merry old soul was he;
He called for his pipe,
And he called for his bowl,
And he called for his fiddlers three.

Every fiddler, he had a fiddle,
And a very fine fiddle had he;
Twee tweedle dee, tweedle dee, went the
  fiddlers.
Oh, there's none so rare
As can compare
With King Cole and his fiddlers three.